S0-HIS-397

Little Shepherd

Mermaid

Mummy

Ogre/Giant/Troll

Old Lady

Robot

Siblings

Space Pirate

Victorian Librarian

Wild Boy

Ancient Temple

Cabin

Castle

Cemetery

City

Coliseum

Desert Oasis

Island

Laboratory

Library

Lighthouse

Magical Forest

Marketplace

Mountain

Mystery Cave

Ocean

Ship

Space Colony

Train Station

Well

For my son, Gideon, on his 3rd birthday

My champion of champions

My strong right arm

Gave his blocks for me to test out this idea

Tells the very best train stories

Fixes everything with his hammer

Curious about, and kind to, dinosaurs

An expert runner and jumper

A very good guy.

Daniel Nayeri

How to Tell a Story

workman

Copyright © 2015 by Daniel Nayeri

All rights reserved. No portion of this book may be reproduced—mechanically, electronically, or by any other means, including photocopying—without written permission of the publisher.
Published simultaneously in Canada by Thomas Allen & Son, Limited.

Library of Congress Cataloging-in-Publication Data is available.

ISBN 978-0-7611-8457-7

Workman books are available at special discounts when purchased in bulk for premiums and sales promotions as well as for fund-raising or educational use. Special editions or book excerpts can also be created to specification. For details, contact the Special Sales Director at the address below or send an email to specialmarkets@workman.com.

Workman Publishing Co., Inc.
225 Varick Street
New York, NY 10014-4381
workman.com

WORKMAN is a registered trademark of Workman Publishing Co., Inc.

Illustrations by Brian Won
Design by Colleen AF Venable

Printed in China
First printing September 2015

10 9 8 7 6 5 4 3 2 1

CONTENTS

HEY, YOU! Yeah, you with the face.

You are holding in your hand a great fantastical machine. An incredible device made of whimsy. It runs on pure imagination—a story engine.

You can use it to make **ANYTHING**

or **ANYPLACE**

or **ANYONE**

in *this* or **ANY OTHER** world.

And to help you on your journey, you've got me.

I'm this book.

Consider me your plot device. Get it? Plot *device*. No? Trust me, that joke *kills* with the librarian crowd. So does this joke: "A guy walks into a library and goes, 'Gimme a burger.' The librarian is confused and says, 'Uh, sir, this is a *library*.' And the guy goes, 'Ooooh. I'm sorry.' Then he whispers, 'Gimme a burger.'"

Still nothing? Okay, fine. You know what? Let's just stick with the plan. No more jokes.

Let's start with the 20 story blocks. You probably didn't even look at them in your rush to open such a good-smelling and shapely book—the kind of book you'd take to parties to show off to all your friends. Those are the building blocks of your great stories.

Notice that each side has a different color background around the image: red, blue, orange, yellow, green, and purple.

WHAT DO THE

Each colored background is loosely associated with a PART OF SPEECH—nouns (people or animals), other types of nouns (things), even more types of nouns (places), adjectives (descriptions or emotions), verbs (actions), and relationships (which, like regular relationships, are a whole bunch of messy things at once).

PEOPLE or ANIMALS	THINGS	PLACES

COLORS MEAN?

PEOPLE or ANIMALS

ACTIONS

ESCRIPTIONS r EMOTIONS

ACTIONS

RELATIONSHIPS

Any time you see this: ● it refers to any image with that color border. For example, I might say:

ROLL 20 BLOCKS AND FIND 1 ● AND 1 ■

Now tell a story with ● as a main character who wants nothing more than to own a ■.

Your story could be about a **GALLANT KNIGHT** setting off in search of his **PRIZED TACO**. Or a **YOUNG LIBRARIAN** who desperately wants her own **LIGHTHOUSE**. The combinations can send you spinning in a million different directions.

But don't forget: The colors are just guidelines. They only exist so that we can communicate better.

Creativity needs a little structure, so it can bounce off of something. But don't let that structure become a prison. If you want to make a blue block a character, go ahead! The blocks can be whatever you want.

As we play with the blocks, we'll explore how stories work. There'll be writing prompts and techniques that storytellers use to make believable characters, tricks to make action-packed scenes, and games you can play just for fun. It's all here to help you exercise your creativity muscles and develop ideas. Maybe you'll write them into short stories or novels someday. And maybe that someday can be soon.

So let's get started.

1. CONFLICT

THERE ARE SO many ways to tell a story that any attempt at creating a formula is bound to fail. Actually, that isn't true. Often, bland and formulaic material is a huge success. But if you want to sell yourself cheap, then you don't need my help to do it.

Vibrant, innovative, powerful, and intriguing stories—those rarely tread the same old ground as others before them. Even if they have a common subject or genre, the best stories find new ways to present themselves. It could be a unique **TURN OF PHRASE**, a mash-up of multiple genres, or a twist ending that no one could have seen coming.

The poet Alexander Pope said it like this:

"True Wit is Nature to advantage dress'd
What oft was thought,
but ne'er so well express'd."

He was saying that clever writing involves finding an emotion or a moment that most people have felt before—and describing it in a way that they have never heard.

Maybe it's a DESCRIPTION OF RAIN.

Or the feeling of LIKING SOMEONE who barely knows your name.

Or the CHOREOGRAPHY OF A FIGHT in a schoolyard.

Expressing these common situations in a unique and interesting way is a major challenge in writing. Often your character just needs to get up, walk across the room, and open a door. The challenge is to make it interesting.

And these blocks can help by giving you practice at creating unexpected combinations.

Let's try it out.

ROLL 10 BLOCKS

Describe a puddle of rain using 1 and 1 .

Was it weird? Did you try something easy for the —like "sad"? Or did you try something more challenging—like "shy"? Now that's interesting. How could a puddle seem shy?

Now, take 2 ■ blocks and describe a scuffle in the schoolyard between them. Yeah, that's right. They're not alive. Doesn't matter. Use your imagination.

Done? Good. Nice work. That was some good warm-up imagining. But now you're ready for a real workout in my imaginasium. See what I did? *Imaginasium? Imagination plus gymnasium?*

I know, I promised no more jokes. That wasn't a joke. That was a portmanteau.

portmanteau **(noun)**

A new word formed by joining two others and combining their meanings.

Feel bad now? You should. The way a portmanteau crashes together two words is a lot like the unexpected combinations of blocks that we've been discussing.

Great sparks of genius can come from the friction of rubbing differing ideas together. Imagination is often a **VIOLENT PAIRING OF OPPOSITES**. It crashes two completely separate ideas together.

Think about that as we move on to conflict, and try to find weird or funny or odd pairings that will help make your creations that much more exciting.

BEGIN at the BEGINNING

Every story has to begin somewhere, and most just start at the very beginning. "Once upon a time, there was a king and queen and they had a beautiful baby"—yadda yadda yadda.

You get the picture. But what is the *beginning*?

When a character is born?

When the bad guy shows up?

Author Darin Strauss, paraphrasing writer Lee K. Abbott, says, **"STORY EQUALS TROUBLE."** He means a story begins when the trouble starts. But how can we know when *that* is?

You can usually find the answer by asking a different question: What does my character **WANT**?

Usually when a character wants something bad enough, they get up and go on a journey to get it. Or they start making decisions they otherwise wouldn't. For example, in the story I mentioned, "There was a king and queen with a baby and they *wanted* very much to protect their newborn baby. So they didn't invite the three witches to her birthday . . ."

Well, let me tell you, their decision not to invite those witches was when all the trouble started.

So if **STORY EQUALS TROUBLE**, the trouble equals the conflict between what we want and what we have. It's the gap between our hopes and our results.

Or to put it another way: Trouble is all the obstacles standing in the way of "happily ever after."

Let's give this a try:

ROLL 20 BLOCKS

Now, let's tell a story from the beginning:

Once upon a time, there was a
who dreamed of visiting a faraway .

Let's stop right here and explore. Do we know why the ● is 💧? Are there enough elements for us to guess when the trouble starts? We know that ● is 💧. We suspect that the goal in this whole story is to travel to the faraway ▲.

Maybe being 💧 is the *reason* ● can't get to ▲.

Or maybe ● hasn't even come across the real trouble in the story. We have to write more to find out!

Okay, back to the story:

> ● *wanted to visit* ▲, *but couldn't get there by* ➡, *because . . .*

Sorry, gotta stop again. Let's go into detail a bit. What is it about ➡ that isn't possible? Is ● physically unable to do it? Or emotionally?

Maybe the *trouble* in this story is the fact that ●

can't manage to ➡ to ▲. If you like that idea, take some time right now to explore that direction. This would be a story about a character's *inner* struggles, since the trouble is coming from fears or inabilities *within* one individual.

Now, let's keep going. Maybe we can find trouble elsewhere:

So ➡ was impossible, but ● was the determined sort and found another way to reach ▲ The journey was long and full of obstacles. As each challenge presented itself, our hero became smarter, stronger, and—to be honest—more and more lonely. After all, a long, hard journey is even longer and harder if you have no one to travel beside.

Though ● continued toward the destination, it started to feel a bit pointless.

Finally, after all the struggle, ● arrived.

Was it LOVELY?
Was it everything it
was HOPED TO BE?

Reader, you may disagree, but I'm going to say…

No. It really wasn't. All those nights of dreaming alone had made an impossible expectation that ▲ *could never live up to.*

But then ● *met* ❷ (pick another ● block), *who had also traveled to* ▲ *in search of something.*

❷ *pointed at a photograph of a* ■ *and said to* ●, *"You know, this particular* ■ *was made a thousand years ago by a love-struck wizard. And if we had it, it would grant all our deepest wishes."*

"Really?" said ●, already feeling as though the entire reason to have traveled here was to obtain ■. "All our wishes?"

"Well, not ALL of them," said ❷. "More like three of them. Three wishes, to be exact."

We can stop here for a moment, because, again, we've got trouble. Two characters suddenly find themselves competing for the same ■. It could be a magic toaster or the heart of someone they love. It could be the throne of a fairy-tale kingdom or the election for a student council president.

And trouble is a great place to start a story.

BEGIN in the MIDDLE

Imagine if we had jumped straight here. Two characters and their conflict. They both have previous lives. Our characters in the previous story, for instance, are from far away. It took a long journey to get to this point. We call a previous life a character's **BACKSTORY**, which is all the experiences a character brings into the story.

We know from before that ● is quite 💧 at the beginning of the journey. But long journeys can change a character. Is ● still 💧?

Or did overcoming all those obstacles along the way change ● somehow for better or worse? Either way, those experiences are a major part of how ● sees the world and behaves when faced with conflicts. Does ● choose to fight or to flee? Negotiate or surrender? You probably have a much better idea because you've taken the time to imagine ●'s backstory.

And now imagine ❷'s backstory. It could be *anything*! And whatever it is, you can be sure that it affects how ❷ will react to this current conflict.

Okay, so we've got two characters with unique backstories in a conflict over a ■, which may or may not be magic and may or may not grant exactly three wishes. You know what? That's a *great* place to start.

As our storyteller, if you start in the middle, then you're going to have to introduce us to the important bits of the backstory as they become necessary.

The ancient Roman poet Horace called this method **IN MEDIAS RES**, which means *"in the middle of things."* He recommended telling stories this way so you can jump straight into the action and fill out the details as you go. Let's see what happens when we begin in the middle . . .

● *had come too far to let a thing like a magic* ■ *slip away.*

"Suppose we shared the wishes," said ❷.

● *considered the offer . . .*

So?

What would the character do?

Based on the backstory, ● might jump on such an offer, or might be suspicious. Maybe it would become a game of intrigue, where both go along with a friendly plan, just waiting for the chance to backstab the other.

The nature of their partnership will be unique to your story, but for now, let's continue the story:

The two worked together to get hold of the magic ■. After a long search, they found it and gave it a vigorous rubbing.

At first, nothing. Just a polished ■.

But then, a shudder. "What was that?" said ❷.

Could have been anything.

"You were moving it," said ●.

"Didn't, I promise!"

Then the ■ began to rumble and sputter on its own, and a great ashy plume erupted into the air.

A genie, giant and horrible, stood before them and spoke, with the booming voice of a storm cloud. ". . ."

Should we make it easy for our characters?

Of course not! We chose to start the story here in the middle because that was when the trouble began.

But what **KIND** of trouble—now that is a good question. What should the genie say?

Suppose the genie says:

> *"How dare you? You have ripped me from my slumber. I will send you to the farthest reaches of the earth!"*

Let's say we banish ● and ❷ to a remote jungle. They will be in a lot of **EXTERNAL** trouble (expressed through cirucmstances outside the character): wild animals, poison plants, heatstroke, hurricanes, you name it. And they both have to find a way to survive.

They can work together. Or they can work alone. But either way, their central goals are not in conflict with each other, because they want the same thing: to get out of the jungle.

Now let's imagine that the genie was not angry but grateful instead:

"Thank you. You have freed me from my prison. I will grant you one wish."

Suddenly ● and ❷ look at each other and realize: They can't *both* have the wish.

For one character to have the wish, the other has to lose it. Even if they got three wishes, who would get the third?

Maybe they would save it? Maybe each would go about enjoying his own first wish (fame! fortune! infinite pie!). But they would both remember the wish they saved—just waiting. It might be a very slow simmering conflict that the two characters resolve decades later, when one tries to sneak off with that last remaining wish.

In that case, the majority of the conflict would be **INTERNAL** (expressed inside the character's mind). Who should have the wish? Who deserves it more?

Over the years, does one character start to feel that a single wish wasn't enough? Does the character feel jealous? Entitled? Enraged?

Those are great *internal* conflicts. But if the two get into a wrestling match over the magic ■, then we have *externalized* it.

If we began the story in the middle, then this will be our first big question: Why are these characters acting this way?

Let's try it with our story.

If you kept your ● block from the previous section, then apply it here. Otherwise:

ROLL THE REMAINING 16 BLOCKS

Pick a ● and imagine the backstory of ● feeling extremely ●.

Does that affect the struggle of who should get the wish? We could go on and describe the conflict between ● and ❷. But let's not forget, we started this story in the middle. At some point, we need to stop and give a little bit of background.

For instance, if ● suddenly felt 💧 when confronted with that last situation, where he had to choose who got the wish, could you tell us why? Why did ● react that way? Often, the reason that a character reacts in a certain way can be found in her backstory.

Maybe ● was spoiled as a child.

Or maybe ❷ was burned once, and is afraid of fire.

Remembering the past, and telling about it, can inform the current trouble, and it can cause all sorts of new conflicts.

BEGIN at the END

Imagine if ● was writing this story, years after everything already happened.

What would ● remember? What would be the important parts? It could begin with ● sitting at a table, writing down the story, or maybe roaming the streets, catching young travelers by the arm to warn them with a parable.

"I had a wish once, a long time ago, when I was much younger. I was just a 💧 ● then, who wanted to travel. When I reached ▲, I met ❷."

It is interesting to wonder what ● thinks of ➋ after all that time. Will ➋ be remembered as an old friend? A villain in disguise? A rival? Maybe a victim of ●'s own regrettable mistakes?

In many ways, the conflict here at the end of the story is internal for ●. By choosing to start here, we've made part of the story about ●'s memory, regrets, and resolutions.

Maybe ● was the only one who survived to tell the tale? Maybe ● is on trial for the disappearance of ➋? Maybe it's a deathbed confession? Or maybe a rollicking adventure told to a bunch of grandchildren?

Starting at the end can be

confusing, because you've got two timelines (old ● telling the story, and young ● getting into trouble), but it can also be rewarding, since it can have twice the conflict (old ● could be telling the story to a detective, acting innocent, while young ● in the story struggles to get that third wish away from ❷).

By the way, the words for jumping around in the timeline of a story are:

Flashback (noun)

The moment in a story when we jump back to see something in the past.

Flash Forward (noun)

Same as flashback, but this time we jump forward to see something happening in the future.

Flash Sideways (noun)

Not really a phrase, but hey, you could invent something. Maybe in a flash sideways, we jump to a parallel universe and see the character eating lizards or fighting orcs or something.

Flash Flash (noun)

This is a phrase I just made up about when a story jumps over to see what the Flash is up to (probably hanging out with Batman). Use sparingly.

So what have we learned?

1. You can start or "open" a story anywhere you like: the beginning, the middle, or the end.
2. An interesting place to start is when the **trouble** begins. **Open on the trouble.**
3. The trouble is when characters come into **conflict** with themselves, with external obstacles, with other characters, or even with their pasts.
4. Conflict is when something or someone stands in the way of what a character **wants.**

So knowing what your character wants is crucial to telling a story and finding the best beginnings. We call that the character's motivation, and we'll talk all about that in the next section.

But for now, let's explore conflicts and openings by playing with the story blocks and following the prompts.

PROMPT

COMBINE

Let's come up with interesting combinations we could use in our stories.

Roll 20

Describe each pairing in a story by saying, "Let me tell you about . . ."

A ▲ where everybody ➡s nonstop.

A ● made entirely out of ■s.

A place where ♥ makes you 💧.

PROMPT

ADAPT

Roll 20

Adapt each of these prompts to be the beginning, middle, or end of a larger story.

"I found it," said the ●, lifting the ■ into the air. "I finally found it."

The siblings agreed never to ➡ again.

The ruler of the ▲ died, and all was right and happy for a long time . . .

MODIFY

Changing one aspect of a character can completely alter the nature of a conflict.

Roll 20

Start a story with:

● wanted ■ or ▲ or ➡ . . .

Any of the last three will work. ● could want a thing, or to go to a place, or to do a certain thing (sail a boat, for instance). Pick one.

Then add:

. . . but it could never be, because ● was too 💧.

Reroll the remaining 17 blocks

Switch out the 💧 block several times. Restate the sentence each time. How is the story different?

LETTER LINK

2–5 PLAYERS • 25 MINUTES

SETUP

Roll 20 blocks.

The player who has most recently finished reading a book goes first.

GAMEPLAY

Each side of the story blocks can represent a variety of things. The first player takes a random block and says a single word that describes an image on one side of the block (the player may choose any side but the first word must begin with the letter *a*). The player then places the block on the table with the chosen side faceup.

For example, the player may place the block showing the image of a rock climber and say the word *adventure*.

The second player then draws another random block and chooses a side with a different color than the previous player and one that can be described with a word beginning with the last letter in the word chosen by the previous player. So in this case, the letter *e*, since that's the last letter in *adventure*.

Gameplay continues, with each player placing a block beside the previous and describing the image with a word beginning with the last letter of the previous player's word.

2. MOTIVATION

PEOPLE WANT.

Some people want things.

Some people want feelings.

Some people want people.

They want love and money and doughnuts and happiness and naps and cars and family and power and beauty and bikes.

Some people want all that stuff.

Some want just a few things.

None want none.

And most want most.

For our purposes, it isn't important *what* things people want. The important part is the *order* in which they want them.

This list of priorities is at the heart of every person's character. It makes up their values or value system.

It is called their *motivation.*

Motivation is the reason people do what they do at any given moment.

Knowing your character's motivation is so important to telling a story that a whole plot could begin like this:

A ● wanted nothing more in this world than a ■.

Remember that? It was the first story we created in the introduction. But did you notice the important phrase this time? ". . . wanted *nothing more* . . ."

That lets us know ●'s order of priorities.

● WANTS:
1. A ■.
2. EVERYTHING ELSE.

●'s own mother could be sick, and if we dangle a ■ within arm's reach, ● would jump for it. That is, unless, over the course of a story, ● could realize that prioritizing a ■ highest above all things is a bad choice—and then maybe ●'s priorities could shift.

For now, ● is experiencing what the philosopher St. Augustine called "disordered love."

It means a person has disordered his list of wants.

We've all seen it happen. A villain disorders her list of priorities and puts "world domination" at the top. A lot of people have to get hurt in order for her to get what she wants.

Sometimes, a hero will be so prideful that he will put himself above everything else. He might even lash out at friends and family if they come into conflict with that self-image.

You can see that the order of the list of wants can make a huge difference in a story. After all, *most* kids want good grades in school, fun activities, and lots of friends. But how we prioritize those things is going to determine the kinds of actions we take.

ROLL 20

Imagine a ● who cares for money more than the law. ● might

steal some coins from a distracted merchant.

But what if ● cares for money more than the law *and* the rights and safety of others? ● might become a bandit on the roadside, capturing travelers and taking their gold.

And what if ● cared for money most of all? More than the law, the safety of others, and even above personal freedom? ● would probably risk everything and rob a heavily guarded bank.

Most people don't agree with that list of priorities, so most people would see ● as a villain.

But some stories try to blur those lines by giving ● a set of motives that we do agree with. For example, what if ● was robbing that bank to help a sick parent? Some people might start to see ● as a hero.

When you're telling a story, a character's motivation answers *why* he does anything. Motivation is important because without it, conflict can get boring pretty quickly.

Want to see? Okay, here's an example.

We need two characters. Let's name them Jaja and Fivehead. They're best friends.

ROLL 20

Pick a ▲.

Okay, they're best friends in ▲.

What do we know so far? Well, we know the two characters have a friendship that they both care about. It's somewhere on their list of priorities. Maybe for Fivehead, the friendship is extremely important. Maybe for Jaja, less so. We don't know that yet. Let's give them some trouble first.

One day in ▲, Jaja and Fivehead were playing a game of catch-the-■ with Jaja's absolute most-favorite-in-the-whole-world ■.

We still don't have conflict, but this is good. We've added something else to Jaja's list. The ■ is a precious thing to Jaja. Okay, now some trouble.

Fivehead was terrible at catch-the-■. The worst, actually, because Fivehead was just too 💧, which makes it difficult to play. But Fivehead always played because Jaja liked it so much.

Hmm. All right. We still haven't added too much trouble. But we do see hints at conflict between Jaja and Fivehead. They seem to have differing priorities.

Jaja loves catch-the-■, the extra-special ■, and the friendship with Fivehead.

Fivehead hates catch-the-■ but cares about their friendship so much that it outweighs the desire to stop playing.

We also know Fivehead feels too 💧 when playing. That could be important later, especially if Fivehead feels 💧 in lots of situations. Okay, this time for real, we need some trouble. Seriously.

Jaja threw the ■ high into the air. Fivehead, feeling 💧, ran back and back, but the ■ was just out of reach as it hit the ground and rolled to a stop at the foot of a giant ●.

I thought I said "Seriously." Let's find the trouble already. This is more like a few random, unlucky things happening.

The giant ● looked mean.

That's good. What else?

The mean giant ● said,
"I will grant you one wish—"

Nope! We did that already. What else? What if the conflict made a little more sense? What if it used some of the characters' motivations, so we're not just seeing a series of random stuff?

The giant ● looked mean but was asleep at the moment, snoring mean snorts. Jaja nudged Fivehead with his elbow and nodded at the ■. "Go get it."

"Me?" said Fivehead. "No way. You get it."

"That's my favorite *," said Jaja.*

"And you'd still have it if we didn't have to play this game all the time."

"You mean I'd still have it if you weren't so *."*

As their voices grew louder, the giant  *began to stir...*

Ooh! Perfect! Now *this* is some serious trouble.

We have the two characters completely unaware that the giant  is about to wake up. That foreshadows a *big* problem.

But even more importantly, Jaja and Fivehead have a kind of conflict that relates to their motivations—they each think the loss of the  is the other one's fault. Now all

that time we spent in the story establishing their feelings about catch-the-■ actually helps us understand the fight.

Jaja thinks it's because Fivehead doesn't value it enough.

And Fivehead thinks it's because Jaja values it *too much*.

Secretly, what they're really talking about is their friendship, and how *it* ranks, too. Fivehead ranks the friendship pretty high, and is willing to play just because Jaja likes it. But Jaja doesn't seem to notice and still prefers the ■ to Fivehead (or so it seems).

The conflict that really matters to these two is:

• FRIENDSHIP FOR FIVEHEAD
• THE ■ FOR JAJA

That's the difference in their motivations.

When the desires and motivations at the heart of a character come into peril, we start to see that person at her most interesting. She becomes fearful, or panicked, or determined, or outraged. She hits emergency mode.

Here's another way to think about motivation in a character.

IMAGINE YOURSELF AT THE CENTER OF A WAGON WHEEL.

Each spoke on the wheel is something you value, something on that priority list we've been talking about. They might be friends and good grades and good looks.

They're all good things to care about. When you are centered in the wheel, you can focus on each of these aspects in your life. But if you slide over to the outer part of the wheel—say, if you start to feel like friends are the *only* thing that matter—then you've turned that good thing in your life into the *only* thing.

You can imagine how it feels to be on the outer rim. You can't control the wheel any longer, because you're no longer at the center. You're spinning out of control.

For the time being, you've made friends number one on your list of priorities and you're hanging on to them for

dear life.

I like that illustration for motivation because people are pretty complicated creatures. A list is a nice simple example, but really, priorities are constantly shifting and changing.

For example, Jaja in our story has a decision to make. Is the friendship with Fivehead more important than his most favorite ? And when the giant awakes, they *both* have a decision to make. Do they want to keep fighting, or should their own safety become the priority?

As circumstances shift in your stories, your characters must constantly decide how to act based on their list of priorities.

So what have we learned?

1. Motivations are the reasons characters do things.
2. Figuring out a character's motivation is figuring out the list of stuff he or she wants most.
3. Values and priorities on that list shift all the time.
4. The most interesting conflicts aren't random. They tend to pit the characters against each other because of their clashing motivations.

Okay, so we talked about conflict and how it can arise from values and motivations. In the next chapter we'll look at a particular type of conflict: conversation. But first, let's explore motives and values by playing with the story blocks and following the prompts.

PROMPT

DEBATE

Roll 10

Oh no! There's a deadly storm on the horizon and Captain Lark has to decide what to do with a ship full of precious ■, the crew of ●, and the magical 2, which can only be used to save one person or thing.

What should Captain Lark save first?

Why? Come up with at least enough stories to argue for saving either the precious ■, the crew of ●, or himself.

PROMPT

VALUE

Stack 6 blocks on top of each other so that 1 of each color is facing you.

This is the list of priorities for a character.

Roll 10

Tell a story about a ● whose values are in the exact order of your stack.

Now rearrange the stack.

How would the ●'s character change with this new order of values?

PROMPT

CHOOSE

Pick 2 blocks

Compare their same-color sides for the activity below.

Which is more important to you?

Feeling or ?

or ?

Being able to or ?

Visiting a or a ?

Owning a or a ?

THE WHY GAME

1–2 PLAYERS • 15 MINUTES

SETUP

This is a cooperative game where 1 or 2 players try to tell a story and must constantly answer the question "why?"

GAMEPLAY

Roll 20. Do not reroll.

The first player begins the story with "There once was a  who was ." Then the first player stops and asks, "But why?"

The second player must then choose another block of the remaining 18 and answer the question using the block to continue the story. After sufficiently answering the question, the second player stops and asks, "But why?"

The first player must then choose a block from the remaining 17 and continue the story.

Play continues until all the blocks are used or neither player can come up with a sufficient answer in the story.

You can play this by yourself. Just stop and ask, "But why?" after every block.

3. DIALOGUE

IN REAL LIFE you can yak about anything.

You can run your mouth nonstop—which is called **LOGORRHEA** (as in the word *diarrhea*).

You can say *uh* and *um* and *like*—which is called **EMBOLALIA** (as in an *embolism*, a big lump of language).

You can say completely random junk that has nothing to do with the situation—which is called **NON SEQUITUR** (Latin for "it doesn't follow").

You can do all that because days are long, and tongues like to wag, and nonsense is a reasonable reaction to the real world.

But stories aren't exactly real life—even if they're about real events. The main difference is that stories have an obligation to be interesting, and life has no such thing.

Every story has to answer the question "So what?"

Why did you just tell me that? So what?

We tell stories to share an experience, to tell a joke, to make a point, to entertain, to explain, or to explore.

We tell stories to others.

We ask for their time and attention.

In exchange we give them something that is worth knowing.

So when we write dialogue—which is characters having a conversation—it shouldn't be filled with logorrhea, embolalia, and non sequitur.

The conversations you choose to tell in a story should deliver *change*. Some *new* information the character didn't know, an argument, a negotiation.

In a sense, all dialogue is a form of conflict.

Let's look at an example:

ROLL 10

● *walked into the room and said, "Hi."*

"Hey," said ❷.

"How's it going?" said ●.

"Good," said ❷.

"I heard that you were searching the ▲, *is that true?"*

"Maybe that's true, and maybe it isn't."

"Were you looking for ■*?"*

"Maybe I was looking for ■. *What do you care?"*

Agggghhhh! I can't take it anymore! Make it stop! Peh! Peh! Ugh. Ugggghhhh!

That was **AWFUL** dialogue. It was boring and unimaginative and superficial. What is it even *doing*? It's just a bunch of words rotting on the page. I can't believe you didn't stop me. I thought we were friends. You should have hit me with something, or called the police.

I can still taste it.

Blech.

Anyway, it's bad because it *wastes time.*

We can cut the:
"Hi."
"Hey."

That's useless. So is the:
"How's it going?"
And the:
"Good."

It's also bad because it has two characters standing someplace like robots. Can you imagine ● and ❷ right now? They're just talking. How often do you walk into a room, arms dangling at your side, and do nothing but talk?

We need ● and ❷ to *do* something meaningful while they talk.

But wait, those aren't the only reasons it's bad. The dialogue is also bad because as ● and ❷ stand nose-to-nose, they each speak back and forth in complete sentences.

How often do you do that? Say your friend asks, "Hey, you mad at me? Is something wrong?"

Do you reply, "Yes, I am mad at you and something is wrong"?

Usually, no. We don't speak in complete sentences. We don't repeat phrases, and we don't volley back and forth—ask, answer, ask, answer—like a gaggle of bobble-headed geese.

So let's go back to that scene and decide what to do with it.

First, we need to figure out what our characters

want from the exchange. What's the motivation?

Let's say ● has heard that ❷ is getting close to finding ■. And let's say ■ is super valuable to both of them.

So now ● is talking in order to figure out what ❷ has discovered. And ❷ is trying to keep it hidden.

That's good. We're making progress.

We used what we know about our two characters' motivations to explore the *inter-personal conflict* they would have.

Now the dialogue will be a subtle game of hide-and-seek. We will have something for them to do physically. And we'll know what each character is secretly trying to achieve in the situation.

Here we go:

● *breezed into the room and pretended not to notice as* ❷ *snatched up the maps to the lost* ▲ *that were spread out on the table.*

"I hear you're searching for the ▲*," said* ●*, leaning over to peek at* ❷*'s notes.*

"Oh yeah? Who told you that?"

Nice. We have action. We have dialogue as negotiation. Now ❷ is trying to distract ● with a question ("Who told you?"), but clever ● doesn't take the bait.

"So you think the ■ is hidden somewhere in the lost ▲," said ●.

"I didn't tell anybody about the ■ but Mr. Glub, back at the traveler's lodge," said ❷.

See what ❷ did there?

It's a statement: I told only one person, Mr. Glub, about my plan.

But it's also a question: How did you get that information? And what have you done to Mr. Glub in order to get it?!

Now we have a hallmark of good dialogue: two people talking past each other. ● wants to know if ❷ has gotten any closer to finding ■. ❷ wants to know how ● even got this far, and what happened to the proprietor of the traveler's lodge.

The scene is full of *subtext*.

SUBTEXT is implied information. Stuff that we understand that isn't directly told to us. In between the lines of dialogue, we see a struggle between ● and ❷ to bend the conversation in the direction of their choosing.

Suppose ● responded to the last line with just a sly shrug.

Now ❷ could read the situation in all sorts of interesting ways.

Maybe ● paid off Mr. Glub to get the information, or maybe something worse. Maybe Mr. Glub is dead. Or

maybe ● and Mr. Glub are friends.

● isn't telling.

❷'s lack of information is a important change in the situation.

Suddenly, ❷ wants to know something that ● wants to keep hidden.

In just four lines of dialogue, we presented two different conflicts between the characters. And the *way* they handle the change lets us know what kind of characters they are.

Suppose ❷ jumps up and threatens violence unless ● explains what happened to Mr. Glub. That would give us some interesting information. First, it says that ❷ might just value Mr. Glub's safety over finding the precious ■.

Remember our look at motivation as a wagon

wheel? Well, in this case, ❷'s motivation has shifted to helping Mr. Glub.

That's a pretty heroic thing to do.

But what if ● implies that Mr. Glub is a hostage until ❷ reveals all the secrets of the map and the search for ■?

Let's try that, and see what happens:

"I didn't tell anybody but Mr. Glub, back at the traveler's lodge," said ❷.

● shrugged and smiled.

"What have you done with Mr. Glub?" said ❷.

"I'll tell you what I've done, if you tell me what you found in ▲."

❷'s teeth ground together. "All right, fine."

Meh. That was *okay*. Nothing great. It went back to the surface, with one character saying, "Give it to me!" and the other saying, "Okay, I'll give it to you!"

It was a whole lot better when the two characters weren't speaking about their motivations out loud. People don't usually do that.

A selfish person doesn't walk around going, "I value myself and my needs above all others!" They just behave that way.

In dialogue, and in interpersonal conflicts, people don't speak at the surface level.

They hide their true goals, because they might be afraid. Or they deceive. Or they

might misunderstand the situation and fool themselves.

For instance, let's revisit that scene:

> *● shrugged.*
>
> *"Wait. What have you done with Mr. Glub?" said ❷.*
>
> *● only smiled.*
>
> *"If anything happens. If you—"*
>
> *❷ couldn't finish. With a sigh, ❷ handed over the maps. "Fine. I'll tell you everything. Just don't hurt him."*

Note that ● didn't say anything this time. It might be a villainous disregard for Mr. Glub's safety. Or maybe ● didn't know what to say. Maybe ● got the information some other way. Now ❷ has completely misunderstood the situation. The desire to save Mr. Glub was so strong that ❷ essentially fell into a self-made trap.

Depending on how you read the situation, ● is either a callous villain or a shrewd trickster. And ❷ is either a noble hero or an overexcited fool.

That's what we want. When dialogue shows conflicting characters engaging with each other, we can say to ourselves, "I've been in that situation, and *wish* I had said something like that," or "I know people *just* like that!"

We have different interpretations, and we want to hear more of the story because we want to see how our impressions play out.

Suddenly, we are *invested* in what happens in the story. We want to know the outcome.

Okay, let's leave ● and ❷ and their race to the precious ■.

So what have we learned?

1. In stories, you have the **obligation to be interesting**. That means no unnecessary dialogue.
2. Good dialogue comes from understanding the characters' **agendas**: what they each want in the moment, what they're hiding, and what they misunderstand.
3. Good dialogue **pits characters' goals against one other** and provides **subtext**, while bad dialogue has them standing in a room speaking their motives out loud.
4. Seeing characters **negotiate conflicts** with each other **invests us** in the outcome, and builds the tension for what happens.

We know conflict and trouble and change are the engines of a good story. We've looked at motivations and how they create conflict between characters. And we've seen how that conflict arises in conversation. In the next chapter, we'll take a look at personal conflict. But for now, let's explore interpersonal conflicts and dialogue by playing with the blocks and following the prompts.

PROMPT

CLASSIFY

Pick 6 blocks

Arrange them into two rows of .

Each of the s is and feels that is very important. Now imagine these two individuals are on a date. How would the conversation go?

Write some dialogue.

Now go back and classify the good and bad dialogue by deleting the parts that ramble and the parts that don't enrich the conflict.

PROMPT

SIMPLIFY

A character might feel a dozen different emotions for any given moment.

Lay out 16 blocks in a grid of 4 × 4, with all the sides up.

For each prompt below, try to imagine the various emotions you would feel. Can you imagine a situation that uses all 16 of them?

Roll the remaining 4 blocks

1. Your mom comes home with a new baby .
2. Your first day is at a haunted school full of monster s.
3. You turn into a gorilla.

TOPPER

2–5 PLAYERS • 30 MINUTES

This is a game of tall tales. Players take on the role of characters bragging about their own experiences, trying to top one another.

SETUP

Each player creates a persona using the following blocks:

= character
= skill
= personality
= item

Players keep these blocks in front of them.

GAMEPLAY

On his turn, a player pulls 1 block and rolls it. Whichever side comes up is the "topic of conversation." The player immediately begins a story (as his character) about how great he is at that topic. He must begin, "Did I ever tell you about that time . . ." and depending on the color of the block, he might say, ". . . that I wrestled a wizard?" or ". . . ate a bathtub full of peas?"

He must continue his tall tale, laying it on thick. Each other player may ask one question to complicate matters, such as, "Wasn't the wizard also a bear?" or "Was it peas, or fleas?"

The player must incorporate the suggestion. He can use his character's skill, item, or personality trait to help tell the story. When the player finishes, the next player says, "Well, that's pretty amazing, but did I ever tell you . . ." and she begins her own story based on the same block, to top the feats of the previous player. The winner of the round is the player who can keep topping the previous story. Then, a new topic block is rolled, and the next round begins.

4. CHARACTER

WHEN YOU HEAR the word *should*, you're often dealing with an ethical or moral obligation. When people say it, they're really saying what they believe in.

What does that mean?

Well, let's give an example.

YOU SHOULD BE KIND.

WHY?

You don't have to be kind to live.
But you *should be* because it's the right thing to do.

WHY?

Because on a selfish level, you want others to be kind to you. But even without the promise of getting something in return, you *should* be kind.

WHY?

Because kindness, as a habit, makes you strong.

WHY?

Because kindness requires patience and self-control and love, even when you don't feel like having any of those things. And so kindness is a heavy weight to lift. But you *should* be kind anyway.

WHY?

Because others have first been kind to you.

Of course, you don't have to agree with me on

this. I think you *should*, but you don't have to. After all, you may not share these beliefs. That's fine. Because when people (or in my case, extremely handsome and intelligent books) use the word *should*, they are trying to answer a much larger question: How should we live?

That sounds like a big question, but it applies to almost every single *should* that people use, even if the subject happens to be very small:

YOU SHOULD DO YOUR CHORES (so that you obey your authority figures, so that you obey laws later on, so that you don't end up an illiterate criminal).

YOU SHOULD DO YOUR HOMEWORK (so that you learn things, and also learn *how* to learn, so that you can grow into someone whose skills and knowledge are always growing, so that you can tackle small and large challenges, and so you don't become an illiterate criminal).

See? The word *should* is another way of arguing that you have an obligation. Remember when I said a story is obligated to be interesting? Well, that is also a *should*.

Stories *should* be interesting because they expect to be heard by others. And if others respect us enough to listen, then we should respect them enough to avoid

wasting their time. Otherwise, they might learn to hate stories and reading, and become angry, and the whole world would turn into illiterate criminals.

Or you might disagree with me and say stories should first be educational or inspiring or whatever.

The point isn't that you should agree with me on kindness or stories. The point is that you should notice when people say *should*. And you should consider whether you *actually* should or not.

ROLL 20

Imagine a village where a powerful governor orders that all people *should* be all the time. And if they're not, then they're sent to be eaten by a mutant .

That's a pretty strong *should*. And it's pretty easy

for us to disagree with it. But what if we imagined a young ● who is told to stop ➡ing, even though ● loves to ➡?

Should ● do it?
What if ➡ing is dangerous?
What if ➡ing could hurt others?

When characters are forced to struggle between what they *want* to do and what they feel they *should* do, then they start to resemble real people—because that is the daily struggle of our own lives.

This is an important part of *characterization*.

CHARACTERIZATION is when we create convincing people in our stories—characters who act and feel real.

Boring, flat characters in your story can develop

into complicated individuals as they experience these sorts of personal conflicts.

ROLL 20

● wants to be accepted by all the other ●s at school, but they're a bunch of petty thieves who take what they shouldn't from the library.

Space treasure-hunters Zeboid and Susan just scored a crate of ■ and are ➡ing away from the evil ●s. They want to escape, but they should probably go back for their partner, who is stranded on the ●s' planet.

● wants to eat more ■, but shouldn't because they're bad for one's health.

A year after a tragic loss, ● should probably "get over it," but ● doesn't want to, and sometimes doesn't feel that one can—or even should—get over such a loss.

That last example was interesting because ● is struggling with the way the world says people should react to a tragedy and the way ● thinks they should react.

At any given time there are many people and communities with conflicting *should* statements. Essentially, these are people looking at a character's list of values and saying the order should change.

Imagine a character who is so desperate for accolades that he will treat others as stepping-stones toward his goals. His values might look like this:

1. *Win awards*
2. *Get praise for winning awards*
3. *Become famous*
4. *Get money*

And then somewhere down there is *Consider the feelings and well-being of others.*

Unless that character is a mustache-twirling cartoon villain, he probably already struggles with how unbalanced his values have become.

Or he might have even fooled himself into thinking his values are just fine. So a better portrait of his internal conflict might be:

His Actual Values

1. *Win awards*
2. *Get praise for winning awards*
3. *Become famous*
4. *Get money*
5. *Etc. (a bunch of other things)*

127. *Consider the feelings and well-being of others*

The Values He THINKS He Has

1. *Win awards and accolades*
2. *Because then he'll give some money to charity*
3. *Fame*
4. *So he can tell people to be nice to one another*

In his head, the character is already justifying his values. He doesn't go around saying, "I have horribly selfish goals in life and disregard others because I'm the villain in someone else's story."

That would be unrealistic. He probably tells himself that if he can just become the most famous, rich, and powerful person, then he can finally make the world better.

It doesn't occur to him that maybe he isn't the best candidate for that job in the first place, and maybe he *shouldn't* be in charge. That is, until he's reminded of it. Say, for example, we showed his uncle teaching him that a good and honest person doesn't harm those around him to get what he wants.

Suddenly the list of values in our character's heart looks like this:

His Actual Values

1. Win awards
2. Get praise for winning awards
3. Become famous
4. Get money
5. Etc. (a bunch of other things)

127. Consider the feelings and well-being of others

The Values He THINKS He Has

1. Win awards and accolades
2. Because then he'll give some money to charity
3. Fame
4. So he can tell people to be nice to one another

What His Uncle Taught Him to Value

1. The feelings of others as well as his own
2. Hard work
3. Achieving good things in his career
4. Fame

Now everything that reminds our character of his uncle also reminds him of how his uncle told him he *should* live his life. He could be the main character of a story about a young actor who has the opportunity to betray his friend in order to get a big part in a movie.

Or the character could be the villainous scrooge who already achieved his fortune but regrets the mistakes of his past.

We all struggle to keep these competing lists of values in balance in our lives, and so do the characters in our stories. Sometimes it's clear that a particular value system is wrong, and sometimes much less so. One lone hero might stand up against the SHOULD STATEMENTS of a misguided community. One sad child may wonder about the right thing to do in a mess of competing voices.

SHOULD is a powerful word. And like all powerful things, it can help or it can harm.

When developing well-rounded characters in a story, let them grapple with all the many *shoulds* in their lives.

So what have we learned?

1. Morals, social standards, and the expectations of others influence us by telling us what we **should** do.
2. Complicated characters have competing values that pull them in different directions between their **wants** and their **shoulds**.
3. Internal conflicts make characters seem **real**.

So far we've focused on trouble in specific situations: where to start the story and how differing goals create conflict externally between people and internally within a character.

Just as we saw with interpersonal conflicts and dialogue, where characters hid their true intentions, characters also hide their true values, even from themselves. In the next chapter, we'll look at the conflicts throughout a story that come together in the climax. But for now let's explore character development by playing with the story blocks and following the prompts.

PROMPT

DEVELOP

Stack 5 ●s on top of each other

This is the family tree of your character, who is the one at the bottom. Tell the story of each person in the family, starting with the great-great-grandparent at the top, going down through all five generations.

PROMPT

REACT

React to some of the *should* statements below by telling the rest of the story.

Roll 15

knows that one should feel once in a while, but to put it plainly, doesn't. Not ever.

"Um, guys, I think we should get outta here," said as they pushed open the door to the .

knew that taking the money hidden under the was wrong. It was wrong, but it had to be done.

WHODUNIT

2 PLAYERS • 15 MINUTES

A murder most foul has occurred. But who could have done it? The Detective must figure out the Who, What, and Where of the case by asking twenty yes or no questions.

SETUP

One person plays the Mastermind. He secretly picks a ● (who), ■ (what), and ▲ (where). These are the "facts of the case." They must each be on a separate block. The Mastermind writes these down on a piece of paper, and keeps it hidden.

Arrange the blocks in a 4 × 4 grid with all the ● sides up.

GAMEPLAY

The Detective begins by asking questions to figure out the Who of the case (the ● that the Mastermind chose). For example, the Detective might ask, "Is the Who human?"

The Mastermind must then provide a sufficient answer ("No, the Who isn't human"). The Detective may rotate any blocks that don't fit (any that are human, for example). These blocks are rotated to the next color in the "facts of the case." So all the human ●s would be turned to ■. In this way, the Detective narrows down the ●s, then the ■s, and ▲s, until she can take a guess at all the facts of the case or runs out of her twenty alloted questions. The Mastermind reveals the piece of paper to see if the Detective was right. If so, she wins. If not, the Mastermind gets away with the crime.

5. PLOT

ONCE UPON A TIME, *there was a silent market in the forest of a lost country. It was silent because the merchants were spirits of long-dead villagers. They needed more gold in order to pay the eternal boatman to ferry them across the river into a place of peaceful rest.*

You might be thinking, "Where's the trouble? Aren't we supposed to start at the trouble?" And you'd be right. Let's present the trouble:

The merchants were unkind.
The merchants were dishonest.
The merchants were vicious.

Okay, so the ghosts were mean. How is that trouble?

Here goes:

The only living creature in the silent marketplace was a little servant girl who had no name. Girl cleaned the stalls.

Girl polished all the merchandise.

Girl hid when travelers in the forest came upon the silent market.

She watched from the trees as they wandered around, as they called out, "Is anyone here?" and, finally, as they perused the trinkets on the tables. Some were honest and paid the price that Girl had written on a leaf next to each item.

Most did not.

This broke the little girl's heart, because she would never be free until each of the spirits could gather enough gold to pay the boatman.

Okay, we're starting to see signs of trouble, and in the meantime, we have lots of helpful information.

Our main character, Girl, is diligent and works for some

scummy ghosts. She *wants* to be free but she needs gold in order to buy her freedom.

One day a young boy wandered into the market. "Is anyone here?" he said. "I'm lost and could pay for a guide to show me the way." When no one answered, the boy sat by a stall and quickly fell asleep.

Up in her tree, Girl felt a familiar prickle by her ear. A spirit whispered, "Kill the soft-belly boy. Kill him and we'd have gold enough to pay the boatman."

Whoa. That escalated fast. And boy do we have trouble.

Will Girl kill for gold?

That depends: Does she value her freedom over the

lives of others? Remember our list of values? What does Girl's list look like?

We'll find out, based on her decision.

She wants to be free of the ghost market, but she knows she *shouldn't* go around murdering people.

Did you catch that *should*?

Girl has an internal conflict to deal with.

Suppose she sneaks up on the sleeping boy with a rock in her hand. We still don't know if she's going to kill him, but we hear the spirits hissing that she *should*. (They're bad spirits, remember.)

But now suppose the

boy startles awake.

Boom.

Now we have some external conflict as well. The boy has gold. Girl needs it.

This would be a fantastic place to show the conversation between the two.

The boy wants to know who she is, why she's sneaking up on him, why she's so weird (after living with ghosts most her life) and—very important—why she's holding a rock.

Girl wants to know if the boy is alone, how much gold he has with him, and—very important—how capable he is of defending himself. Maybe she could just knock him down and grab the gold or something.

AFTER ALL, GIRL'S LIST OF VALUES MIGHT BE:

1. *Being a person who doesn't kill*
2. *Her freedom*
3. *Being a person who doesn't steal*

Meaning, she might have no problem taking the soft-belly boy's money if he proves to be a spoiled brat. But she wouldn't kill him, because she knows that's wrong (even if it means she can't have her freedom).

That would be good dialogue. But then what? We've got ourselves a strong beginning, some trouble, and some interesting conflicts that pit our characters against each other based on their desires and the expectations of others.

Where do we go after that?

Dear Reader, it is my pleasure to tell you that we can go wherever we want.

ROLL A BLOCK

Did you roll a ●?

Make the boy a secret member of a group of ●s.

Or add a third character, a ❷ who happens upon them mid-argument.

Did you roll a 💧?

Consider how the dialogue would shift if Girl or the boy felt 💧.

Is this new, third character ➡?

Great. Describe a scuffle using ➡.

Put a ■ in the scene by having Girl try to sell it to the boy. Maybe she tries to trick him into thinking it's magic and it will guide him out of the woods.

Did you roll a ♥? Alter their relationship to be about ♥.

If you'd like to end the story right now, just have everybody get what they want.

The boy hands over the coins.

The girl points him to the nearest exit.

Done.

NO MORE TROUBLE MEANS NO MORE STORY.

But suppose we wanted to tell a full story. Then we'd need to find a way to get our character or characters off onto a larger adventure, a journey.

Plot (noun)

The bones of the story.
The stuff that happens.

Ideally, a plot feels a lot like a roller coaster. You start out with a bit of action:

The cars rattle into the starting blocks, people still screaming, laughter, a few faces still green.

That gets us excited about what's to come. Then we get some background:

The bored attendant speaks into the microphone. "Wellllll-come to the Barf-in-ator, the fastest coaster in the world. Please keep your hands and feet in the car at all times."

The background leads into the development. This is usually when we really dig into the characters and see them act out their motivations.

The coaster is slowly clicking up the massive hill.

We see the crest.

We approach it.

People start squirming.

Some scream early.

It was all building to this moment.

Can't go back now.

It's tipping.

Look at that view.

AGGGHHHH!

THAT'S THE CLIMAX.

In a story, the climax is the moment when all that conflict we've been developing comes to a conclusion.

Sometimes it's explosive. A gunshot. The ending of a friendship. A horrible accident. Sometimes it's just a quiet resolution to be better. Sometimes the climax is an epiphany, a moment of inspiration that changes how our character sees the world.

In our earlier story, the climax would be the moment that resolves whether or not Girl wins her freedom from the ghost market and the boy gets out of the forest.

Maybe they both do. Maybe just one. Or maybe neither ends up getting what they want.

The question has to be resolved, however, because the climax is all about change. It's about the moment that the characters finally come face-to-face with what they've been wanting from the start. And either they get it or they don't.

The important part is that *change*. When we're screaming down the slope of the Barf-in-ator, there is no going back up the ramp. We're either going to barf, or we're not. But either way, we're getting to the bottom of that ramp.

And after the climax, when we've conquered the machine, or we've got chunks of hot dog all over our shirts, the cars roll us on a flat track for a while. We laugh and compare notes, and wrap it up.

That's the ending of the story of the Barf-in-ator.

That's the narrative arc.

OPEN ON TROUBLE.

DEVELOP THE CONFLICT BY SHOWING HOW IT RELATES TO THE CHARACTERS' MOTIVATION AND VALUES.

PUT THOSE VALUES IN DANGER.

BRING THE CONFLICT TO RESOLUTION.

That's a very basic arc.

ROLL 20

Start with a  or . What does this character want? Pick any color block. A desire can be anything.

Why can't the character have it?

How does the character try to get it?

Does it work?

Keep in mind, this formula isn't meant to be followed strictly. It's only here to highlight a useful piece of information: *Your story is going to come out of your characters' desires*. The plot is a series of moments where the characters struggle to reach their goals.

At the climax, when the character is going to achieve the goal or fail, we should be riveted, screaming for the result we want, as if we were riding on the Barf-in-ator.

To do that, the plot can't be a bunch of unrelated events. It can't have the "list problem."

Imagine if we told a story like this:

ROLL 20

Once, there was a ● who wanted nothing more in this world than to visit a faraway ▲. Then ● met ❷.

"Hi. I really wish I could get to ▲."

"Cool," said ❷. "Wanna play catch-the-■?"

So they played for a while, and then  *went home and dreamed of* *.*

The next morning,  *heard a crash. It was an invasion of*  *aliens.*

Bah! That's enough. I thought you were gonna stop me! Didn't we already discuss this? Anyway, that is a *terrible* story, even though it includes aliens and motivations and action. That's because it's just a list of things that happened strung together with "and then." There is no reason for one thing to follow the other.

It's random.

It's coincidence.

You might as well roll dice that have pictures on them. You know, *without* the color-coded system on our story blocks. Just random dice.

A story like that could start and stop anyplace. It's the way someone tells about the events of their day when they're super bored and uninterested.

"I went to school. Then I had lunch. Then I read about cell growth. Then I found five dollars."

Okay. Great. Good for you. That bit about the five dollars had my heart racing for a minute there.

To avoid the "list problem," you have to know what your character wants and what is standing in the way—whether it's a circumstance, a personal flaw, an inner conflict, or an antagonist.

Antagonist (noun)

Someone or something standing against the protagonist (the main character).

From there, you can imagine and predict the plot. Because each moment should lead from the previous. The character wants X, but can't have it because Y. So what does the character do? Something else. But that doesn't work either, because Z.

You can imagine how complicated it can get as your character meets others (with their own conflicting goals), discovers new challenges, and maybe begins to question his or her own values. A story can be about *anything*.

Think of your climax as a simplifying moment, at least because it answers the question "Will our  get what he's after?"

Maybe so. Maybe not. Maybe by then it won't even matter.

Say a story started like this:

Let me tell you about the time I bet a rancher that I could lasso his meanest bull with nothing but dental floss.

Cool. We can wander all over the place, but at some point, we want to see that bull smacking around the overconfident narrator.

The climax resolves the trouble that started our story, and then the characters move on. They change. In this case, they have horn marks on their backside.

So what have we learned?

1. A plot is a series of conflicts in a story.
2. One good structure for a plot is to start with a conflict faced by a character, develop the character's motivation, and build toward a climax.
3. The events leading to the climax shouldn't be random. They should complicate the situation for the character, who's struggling toward a goal.
4. The climax takes all that complication and pressure and blows it all up into the simple answer to one question: Will the character get what she wants?
5. The climax changes our character.

In the next chapter, we'll look at how these collections of conflicts come together to form themes in storytelling. But for now, let's explore plot and story structures by playing with the story blocks and following the prompts and game.

PROMPT

PREDICT

Roll 20

Pick any two of the elements below. Imagine the types of conflicts that might arise if the two came together in a story.

A car full of angry ■s.

The only person in the world who can ➡.

An island of living ■2s.

A 💧 thief.

A city where ♥ is illegal.

A bear that can't stop ➡2ing.

Ghosts of famous ●s.

The Greek god of 💧2.

A ▲ full of sad clowns.

PLOT BUILDERS

2–4 PLAYERS • 25–45 MINUTES

SETUP

Give each player 5 blocks.

GAMEPLAY

Each player rolls and sets their 5 blocks faceup in front of them, regardless of color. They cannot reroll the blocks from here.

The person with the most ● sides goes first. She places one of the ●s in the center of the table and says, "There once was a ● who . . ."

From here the player improvises a story. The goal is to incorporate all of her blocks into the tale. She must develop each block using a minimum of one sentence. But don't rush! This is not a competitive game. The idea is to create a satisfying story for all players.

Another player may interject if she can weave one of her blocks into the current story without interrupting the sense or flow of the tale.

The storyteller can also pass the story to the player on her left if she gets stuck or starts to ramble.

The first player to finish the story with a satisfying climax and ending, having used all of their blocks, is the winner. But really, everyone is the winner for having heard a great story.

6. THEME

IF YOU'VE MADE IT this far, then you're a good person and I love you. And you've probably gathered that this is a book about one thing:

Conflict.

Which is another way of saying: Trouble.

Which is another way of saying: Story.

It's the subject of this book.

But what's the theme?

A *theme* is a unifying idea at the center of a story. A central idea.

It's a bit difficult to identify a theme in an instructional book, but let's try. What are some of the conflicts at the heart of this book (me)? What does the book itself want? I'll tell you. I want:

To talk about storytelling in an interesting way.

To understand basic craft without becoming a tool

for formula.

To exercise imagination like it's a muscle.

To make room in each chapter for instruction, practice, and play.

All of these are conflicts. That last one is a major conflict for a book as thin as I am. What do I emphasize in the little space I have? If you look at each chapter, you'll see a dedication to learning, practicing what we've learned using the prompts, and then a game.

So the theme, then, is about valuing discipline and whimsy equally.

Okay, so that's me. But what about other stories? Theme is the idea at the center of all the various conflicts we see throughout a story. In a story with lots of characters, each character might show a different aspect of the main idea.

Each character, each moment in a story, has a particular relationship with the central idea. This is getting abstract, so let's pause for a second and look at the story blocks.

You know that ♥ side?

The one we haven't used very much at all?

You probably thought I forgot about it.

Think again, punk. I'm a book, not a clown. I remember things for a living.

The ♥ sides have been waiting all this time for us to discuss *theme*.

Take a look at a few of them.

They show relationships or situations.

Each of these relationships could be expressed a hundred different ways—even in the same story.

One of my favorite stories is about a boy who decides he wants to leave civilized society and go live in the trees. The story is called *The Baron in the Trees*.

The theme is a set of conflicts throughout the boy's life that result from his refusal to become civilized. *Huckleberry Finn* has a similar theme, actually.

FRIENDSHIP

LONGING

FEELING ALONE

FAMILY

RICH & POOR

FEUDING

Another story might be about the conflicts that people face when they travel into the wilderness and brave the dangers of the natural world. Books like *Giants in the Earth* and *Little House on the Prairie* both have that theme.

Another story might be about a family just trying to live with each other—a theme in *The Brothers K* by David James Duncan and *Anne of Green Gables.*

The set of conflicts in a story not only push the plot along but also come together to form the theme. Here's an example:

ROLL 20

● and ❷ are best friends who dream of going to the big city so that ● can ➡ all day long and ❷ can ➡2.

Okay, we've got a basic setup with two characters and some vague idea of what they might want.

Now pick a ♥.

How would you explore the possible conflicts in the story if you were imagining it with ♥ as the theme?

It's not an easy question.

One way to answer it is to ask:

How does ● feel about ♥?

And how does ❷ feel about ♥?

Now pick a ♥2.

Can you imagine the story of ● and ❷ off in the big city with ♥2 as the central idea for their story? You can imagine lots of different ways to explore a particular theme. For instance, could you tell the story of

● and ❷ as they experience conflicts that relate to ♥ in a funny way? What about a very serious approach?

It's amazing to think of all the various Romeo and Juliet stories. They all have the same basic plot and conflicts, but some versions want to explore the theme of tragic love, and some want a comedic romp where Romeo and Juliet win in the end.

If you were telling a *Romeo and Juliet* story, how would you tell it?

So what have we learned?

1. The collection of conflicts in a story form a **theme.**
2. The themes of a story are its **central ideas.**

PROMPT

REMIX

Roll 20

There once was a monster who roamed near a remote ▲ where there lived a thousand ●s.

Tell the story above as one of the following styles:

Comedy
Gothic/horror
Fantasy
Adventure
Romance
Parable
Sci-fi
Courtroom drama

Think about each of these styles and identify some of the common themes you have noticed within it.

PROMPT

RECOUNT

Make a grid of 6 ●s

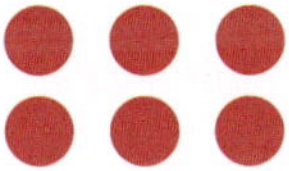

These are the weirdos I met at summer camp. By the end of the summer, one of them would become my best friend. One my mortal enemy. One would go home early. And one would wind up dead.

Build out from each character with other blocks to continue to tell about their back-story, personality, motivation, and plot.

THAT'S IT! We're done. Well, sort of. We're just ready to start in earnest. But look at all the stuff you've got in your head! I'm in there right now, so I can tell you, it's crowded in here.

You're full of great ideas about trouble and characters with big dreams, and how our values shape us, and all the many conversations we have had as storytellers across time and space.

And now it's your turn.

If you need a second, just clear your throat. But then look up. Look your audience in the eye, because you've got something interesting to tell them. It might be the best story they've ever heard.

You've practiced.

And you've listened.

And now you can say, *Hey, let me tell you a story worth knowing . . .*

Aging

Balancing

Beauty

Big & Small

Caring for Others

Longing

Disaster

Family

Distance/Far Apart

Feuding

Friendship

Good vs Evil

Being Lost

Rich & Poor

Secrets

Feeling Helpless

Teamwork

Disorder

Being Identical

Feeling Alone

Apple

Briefcase

Birthday Cake

Car

Flamingo

High-Tech Gadget

Key

Magic Lamp

Nice Clothes

Painting